Hope & Luna

A Modern Fable

Charles J. Orlando

one room press

Los Angeles, CA

This book is an original publication of
One Room Press
A division of Loft 327, Inc.
333 S Grand Avenue, Suite 3310, Los Angeles, CA 90071
oneroompress.com

ORP Ebook / Paperback Edition 2023
10 9 8 7 6 5 4 3 2 1

1. Interpersonal Relations   2. Adult Fiction
3. Consciousness & Thought   4. Marriage & Adult Relationships

PB ISBN: 978-0-9979029-6-9
EB ISBN: 978-0-9979029-7-6

Printed in the United States of America.

For my fish.
For my chicken.

Clear skies ahead.

Introduction

. . . .

The Fable
of Hope & Luna

Have you ever felt the weight of the world pressing down yet still found the strength to smile? Have you ever faced heartbreak only to find a hidden reservoir of resilience? In those moments, in those feelings, you've met Hope.

Hope isn't just a character in this story; she's the reflection in your mirror on those early mornings when the world is still asleep, and you're gathering the courage to face the day. She's the voice in your head that whispers, "You can," when everything else screams, "You can't."

In Hope's story, through every twist and turn, Luna, Hope's diary, has been right by her side—not just as a diary, but as a silent witness to Hope's journey. Luna's job is one she enjoys: empathetically absorbing every tear, echoing every laugh, and holding all the weight of every unspoken emotion.

From a young age, Hope found solace in Luna's pages. A gift on her twelfth birthday, Luna quickly became Hope's confidante, capturing her dreams, aspirations, and the intricate dance of her life. As Hope navigated the challenges of growing up, Luna bore witness to her first crushes, the joy of school successes, and the sting of teenage heartbreaks. Their nightly, calming ritual saw Hope pouring her heart out, finding clarity amidst the chaos of adolescence.

Hope's bond with Luna was evident in the diary's physical appearance. Over the years, Luna's once-pristine pages became filled with Hope's neat handwriting, doodles in the margins, and an occasional tear stain. Once a simple shade of blue, Luna's cover was adorned with stickers and quotes that resonated with the early parts of Hope's journey. And as diary pages ran out and new diaries appeared, Luna was always Luna: Hope's inner voice on the external page. When Hope felt the warmth of sunny days or the chill of stormy nights, she turned to Luna. When life presented its predictable rhythms or threw unexpected challenges, Luna's pages offered solace.

Hope's journey is a combination of highs and lows, moments of certainty, and phases of doubt. And through it all, Hope is and remains a reflection of our collective experiences. As you turn each page of her story, you might find yourself thinking, "This feels familiar." This is because Hope's journey isn't just hers; it's yours. It's ours. It's a tapestry woven from threads of shared experiences, dreams, fears, and triumphs. So, as you delve deeper into her world, remember: every tear, every laugh, every decision Hope makes reflects the myriad emotions and choices we've all faced.

Through her and the silent pages of Luna, discover, reflect, and embrace the Hope that resides within you.

Charles J. Orlando

Chapter 1

. . . .

Reflections

Growing up, Hope's home was filled with an ever-changing cacophony of energy and emotions. There were days of laughter, where the house echoed with joy, and days of silence, where unspoken words hung heavily in the air. Her parents, while loving, had their own set of challenges. Their relationship was a complex dance of love, misunderstandings, reconciliations, and silent treatments. Young Hope observed, absorbing lessons even when she didn't realize it.

School was an escape, a place where Hope could be herself. She formed close bonds, especially with her friend, Nikki. They shared secrets, dreams, and the kind of laughter that only true friends understand. It was Nikki who introduced Hope to the world of romance, lending her novels filled with passionate love stories. These tales painted a picture of love that was intense, all-consuming, and often fraught with challenges. Hope, with her vivid imagination, often found herself lost in these narratives, dreaming of her own love story.

But the reality was different. Her middle school crush, a boy named Jake from her class, barely noticed her. The heartbreak of unrequited love was a new emotion, but Hope, ever resilient, took it in stride. Hope loved and trusted Nikki, but there are some things that even best friends can't share. Hope penned her deepest thoughts and feelings in Luna, her diary.

Dear Luna —Jake smiled at me today, but just for a second. Does he even know I exist? Nikki says there's someone out there for everyone. I wonder when I'll find my someone.

Luna loved being there for Hope. Luna listened, accepted, and wanted only the best for her.

Patience, dear Hope. Every heart has its own rhythm, its own time. Yours will find its match.

Hope couldn't hear Luna, but that was okay. Hope was very young, and there was plenty of time.

As the years went by, Hope's understanding of love evolved. Puppy love turned to teenage love, and she began to see that relationships weren't just about grand gestures or intense emotions. It was also about understanding, compromise, and growing together. But these lessons came over time and with their own challenges, setting the stage for the relationships that would come to define her happiness and sense of self-worth in her adult life.

With each entry in Luna, Hope chronicled her journey. And Luna, in her silent, steadfast way, offered comfort, wisdom, and a listening ear. Through the pages of Luna, Hope's journey of self-discovery unfolded, one chapter at a time.

Chapter 2

Brad

The college campus was alive with the energy of new beginnings. First-year students like Hope always buzzed with a mix of excitement and nervousness. During one of the beginning-of-the-year college parties, Hope's eyes met Brad's amidst the laughter and chatter.

Brad had an aura that was hard to ignore. Tall, with a confident stride and a smile that seemed to light up the room, he was the center of attention wherever he went. Their initial conversations were effortless. They talked about everything—from their favorite books to their dreams for the future. Hope felt a connection, a spark she hadn't felt before.

As days turned into weeks, their relationship deepened. They spent countless hours together, studying, watching movies, and exploring the city. But as the initial euphoria waned, Hope started noticing the red flags.

Brad, for all his charm, had a controlling side. He'd decide where they'd go, what they'd do, even what Hope should wear. He'd make plans and cancel them last minute, leaving Hope disappointed and waiting. Their relationship seemed to be on his terms, and Hope, eager to make it work, often found herself sidelining her own needs.

Dear Luna — Brad can be so wonderful, making me feel like I'm the only person in the world. But there are times when I feel overshadowed, lost in his world. Why do I keep sidelining my own needs? Is this what love is supposed to feel like?

Luna, absorbing Hope's words, wished she could hug her friend.

Oh, dear Hope. Love should be a dance of two souls, not one leading and the other merely following. Remember your worth.

Hope couldn't hear Luna, but Hope's friends noticed the changes, also. Nikki, ever the protective friend, voiced her concerns. "He's not right for you, Hope. You're losing yourself in this relationship." But Hope defended Brad, attributing his behavior to stress and the pressures of college.

However, as finals approached and the pressures mounted, Brad's behavior became more erratic. Their arguments grew frequent, often over trivial matters. Hope felt like she was walking on eggshells, constantly trying to avoid any situation that might upset Brad.

One evening, after a particularly heated argument, Hope sat alone in the college library, tears streaming down her face. She realized that while she cared about Brad, their relationship affected her mental and emotional well-being.

Dear Luna — I really like Brad, but at what cost? I miss the old me... the one who laughed freely and dreamt big. What happened to her?

Feeling the weight of Hope's sadness and confusion, Luna whispered back in the silence.

You're still here, Hope! Sometimes, we need to step back to see the bigger picture. Trust your instincts and remember your dreams.

Hope couldn't hear Luna, but she made the hard decision to end things with Brad anyway. And it was one of the most difficult choices Hope had ever made.

Chapter 3

. . . .

Malcolm

The end of her relationship with Brad left Hope with mixed emotions. There was the lingering pain of heartbreak, but also a newfound sense of freedom and self-awareness. As time passed and the wounds began to heal, Hope decided to venture into the world of online dating. It was a realm she hadn't explored before, and meeting someone outside her immediate circle was both exciting and nerve-wracking.

It was on one of these apps that she came across Malcolm's profile. His bio was witty, his interests aligned with hers, and their online conversations flowed effortlessly. They shared jokes, exchanged stories, and soon decided to meet in person.

Their first date was at a downtown café. The ambiance was perfect: soft lighting, gentle music, and the aroma of freshly brewed coffee. Malcolm was just as charming in person as he was online. They talked for hours, losing track of time. Hope felt a connection, a sense of familiarity that was comforting.

However, as they continued to date, Hope noticed a recurring theme in their conversations. Malcolm often spoke about his ex-girlfriend, recounting their shared memories and the pain of their breakup. While Hope tried to be understanding and supportive, she couldn't shake off the feeling that she was living in the shadow of Malcolm's past.

Dear Luna — Malcolm is kind, attentive, and we have so much in common. But I can't help but feel like a rebound. Every conversation somehow circles back to his ex. I want to be understanding, but it's hard not to feel like a placeholder.

Luna, sensing Hope's frustration and pain, responded silently.

Love should be about the present and future, not anchored in the past. Trust your feelings, Hope. You deserve someone who sees and values you for who you are.

Hope couldn't hear Luna. And Hope felt like a training ground for Malcolm's growth.

Hope tried to address the issue, gently suggesting that Malcolm might not be ready for a new relationship. But Malcolm was insistent, assuring Hope he was over his ex and that what they shared was genuine. Hope wanted to believe him, but the doubts lingered.

One evening, after another date dominated by stories of Malcolm's past, Hope decided to take a step back. She realized that while Malcolm might be a great person, he wasn't emotionally available for a new relationship. Was that her fault? Wasn't she important enough to see as valuable?

Dear Luna — I've decided to end things with Malcolm. Why doesn't he see me for me? Why is everything about his ex? Aren't I enough?

Luna, ever the comforting presence, whispered back.

You are more than enough, Hope. Sometimes, it's not about your worth but the other person's readiness. Remember, you deserve a love that celebrates you in the present, not one tethered to the past.

Hope couldn't hear Luna. And all Hope could feel was that she wasn't enough.

Chapter 4

. . . .

John

The bustling corporate world was a far cry from the college campus Hope had left behind. As she settled into her new job, she found herself surrounded by a diverse group of colleagues, each with their own stories and experiences. Among them was John, a colleague from a different department.

Their initial interactions were purely professional, discussing projects and deadlines. But as the weeks passed, they bonded over shared interests outside of work. From their love for indie music to their mutual appreciation for art, their conversations grew richer and more personal.

Lunch breaks turned into coffee dates, and soon, Hope and John were spending more time together outside of work. Their chemistry was undeniable, and it wasn't long before their colleagues started teasing them about their budding romance. However, as their relationship progressed, Hope sensed John's hesitance to commit. Their dates, while fun and spontaneous, lacked depth. John skillfully avoided conversations about the future, and Hope felt stuck in a loop of casual dates without any clear direction.

Dear Luna — John is fun, spontaneous, and we have a great time together. But I can't help but feel like a friend with benefits. I want more, a deeper connection, a commitment. But every time I bring it up, he changes the topic. Am I asking for too much?

Sensing the shift in Hope's tone and the absence of her dreams, Luna responded with a hint of worry.

Hope, you've always dreamed big and sought depth in connections. Trust your feelings. If something feels amiss, it probably is. Remember the dreams and aspirations you once shared with me.

But Hope couldn't hear Luna. Hope asked John to address her concerns, hoping for clarity. But John's responses continued to be vague, with promises of "let's see where this goes." Hope felt like she was in limbo, unsure of their relationship status.

One evening, after another non-committal response from John, *he* was the one who ended the relationship. "You're just too demanding and want too much," John said.

Dear Luna — I guess I was just a booty call? What happened with him, and why wasn't I worth investing in? I keep finding these guys who don't want anything but fast-moving and casual times. I'm looking for my person. What gives?

With a growing concern for Hope's well-being, Luna whispered back.

Hope, seeing you question your worth based on fleeting relationships pains me. You've always been so much more than the roles you play in these relationships. I miss the Hope who dreamt big and believed in herself. Please remember her.

But Hope couldn't hear Luna. Instead, Hope tried to figure out what she was doing wrong.

Chapter 5

. . . .

Andy

The city's vibrant nightlife starkly contrasted with Hope's daily corporate routine. On weekends, she'd often head out with friends, exploring new places and meeting new people. On one such night, amidst the pulsating beats of a downtown club, she met Andy.

Andy was different from anyone Hope had ever met. He was a musician, passionate about his craft, and had an air of mystery that Hope found intriguing. Their initial conversations tingled with stories of his travels, gigs, and dreams of making it big in the music industry.

Hope was drawn into Andy's world as they began dating: late-night jam sessions, impromptu weekend road trips, and a life free from the constraints of a 9-to-5 routine. It was exhilarating, and Hope felt like she was living a dream.

However, as the weeks went by, she began to see the cracks in the facade. Andy, for all his charm, was unpredictable. He'd disappear for days, only to return with vague explanations. He was evasive about his past, and Hope began to feel that there was a side to him she didn't know.

Dear Luna — Andy's world is so different from mine. It's exciting but also chaotic. I mean, I never know where I stand with him. There are moments of pure bliss but also days of uncertainty. Is this what love is supposed to feel like? I'm so confused.

Sensing the whirlwind of emotions Hope was going through, Luna responded with gentle wisdom.

Love can be an adventure, Hope, but it should also be a place of safety and connection. Trust and transparency are its cornerstones. Remember, you deserve clarity and consistency.

Hope couldn't hear Luna. And as Hope tried to understand Andy and his world, she made excuses for his flighty, flaky behavior. She'd defend him to her friends, attributing his actions to the pressures of his career. But deep down, she knew something was off.

One evening, after another unexplained absence from Andy, Hope confronted him. The conversation that followed was intense. And while Hope wanted to be understanding and supportive, Andy ended things and labeled Hope "high maintenance."

Dear Luna — I got dumped again. Andy decided he wanted his freedom and not me. Seems to be a running issue with all these guys. Does anyone want a regular commitment? Just something normal and maybe even a little predictable?

Feeling the weight of Hope's repeated heartbreaks, Luna whispered with compassion.

Hope, love isn't about settling for less than you deserve. Your heart seeks a connection that's genuine and steadfast. Don't lose faith. Your journey is leading you to the love you truly deserve.

Hope couldn't hear Luna. Instead, she questioned her own worth in the maze of fleeting relationships.

Chapter 6

. . . .

Jeff

After her whirlwind experience with Andy, Hope craved stability. She yearned for a grounded relationship where she felt secure and valued. As fate would have it, she reconnected with Jeff, an old college friend.

Jeff was the epitome of familiarity. They shared history, common friends, and countless memories from their college days. Their conversations were filled with nostalgia, reminiscing about old times and shared experiences. As they began dating, Hope felt a sense of comfort she hadn't felt in a long time.

As their relationship deepened, Hope felt she had finally found someone who truly understood her.

Jeff was attentive, caring, and always made Hope feel special. They talked about the future, made plans, and Hope genuinely believed she had found her life partner in him.

However, as time passed, Hope noticed subtle changes in Jeff's behavior. He became more secretive, often guarding his phone and becoming defensive when Hope asked about his plans—their once open and transparent relationship brimmed with evasions and half-truths.

Dear Luna — Something's changed with Jeff. He's distant, mysterious. I trust him, I guess, but I can't shake off this nagging feeling that something's not right.

Feeling the undercurrents of Hope's unease, Luna responded with a gentle caution.

Trust is the foundation of love. Always listen to your intuition, Hope. It's there to guide and protect you.

Hope couldn't hear Luna. One evening, Hope's worst fears were confirmed. A mutual friend, hesitant and apologetic, shared with Hope that they had seen Jeff out with another woman on multiple occasions. Pictures confirmed it was Jeff, and the revelation was a gut punch. Hope confronted Jeff, and after initial denials, he admitted to having an affair.

Dear Luna — This pain is unbearable. I can't breathe! Jeff's betrayal has shattered my trust, not just in him but in love itself. How could he? After everything we shared, how could he throw it all away?

Luna, in her attempt to silently absorb the depth of Hope's pain, whispered back with compassion.

Betrayal is a reflection of the betrayer, not the betrayed. You are deserving of unwavering love and trust, Hope. Remember your worth, even when others fail to see it.

Hope couldn't hear Luna. Instead, she was enveloped in a storm of emotions, trying to make sense of the betrayal and her part in it.

Charles J. Orlando

Chapter 7

· · · · · · · · · ·

Martin

Hope's relationship with Jeff left her in a vulnerable state. She wasn't actively seeking a relationship, but fate had other plans. At a work conference, she met Martin. He was charismatic, intelligent, and they shared an undeniable chemistry. Their conversations flowed, and by the end of the conference, they had exchanged numbers.

Their relationship began innocently enough — texts became phone calls, and phone calls became meet-ups. Martin was attentive, always eager to listen to Hope's stories, dreams, and fears. He made her feel special.

Dear Luna — There's something about Martin. He understands me in a way that no one else does. But there's also a shadow, a secret he's not sharing.

Luna, sensing the hesitancy in Hope's words and feeling the growing distance between them, responded with a gentle caution.

Trust your intuition and seek clarity, Hope. Remember: you are strong, and your gut never lies. Pay attention to your inner voice!

Hope couldn't hear Luna. As weeks turned into months, the nature of their relationship began to change. Their meetings were always discreet, often in out-of-the-way places. Martin was evasive about his personal life, and Hope began to suspect that he was hiding something.

One evening, her suspicions were confirmed. While waiting for Martin at a cafe, she overheard a conversation where people referred to Martin as "a married man." The revelation was a shock. All the pieces fell into place—the secrecy, the discreet meetings, the hiding.

Dear Luna — Martin made me feel alive, but at what cost? Every stolen moment, every secret message... it's a reminder of the lies we're living. I'm stealing someone else's husband!? I can't do that. I know what it's like when someone cheats on you. Don't I deserve a love that's real and not one that's hidden in the shadows?

Feeling the weight of Hope's pain, Luna whispered back with deep concern.

Love shouldn't be built on deception, Hope. You deserve honesty and transparency. Remember your worth and the dreams you once aspired to.

Hope couldn't hear Luna. Confronting Martin was one of the hardest things Hope had ever done. He admitted to being married, explaining that he felt trapped in his marriage and found solace in his relationship with Hope. The relationship ended, leaving Hope with mixed emotions — anger, betrayal, and guilt.

Dear Luna — I'm an idiot! All the signs were there, just like with Jeff, but I ignored them... again! Now I was helping someone cheat!? How did I end up here, in a relationship with a married man?

Luna, with a heavy heart and growing worry for Hope's well-being, responded softly.

Hope, sometimes the heart seeks comfort in places it shouldn't. Learn from this, and remember the dreams and aspirations that once fueled your spirit.

Hope couldn't hear Luna. Instead, regret, emptiness, and self-doubt consumed her.

Chapter 8

. . . .

Awakened

The weight of her past relationships pressed heavily on Hope's shoulders. Each was a lesson, a scar, a memory that shaped her perception of love and self-worth. But the relationship with Martin served as the final straw. The realization that she was involved with someone already committed to another was a jolt to her system. It wasn't just about being deceived; it was a glaring reflection of the patterns she had unknowingly set for herself. This was her moment of reckoning.

Dear Luna — How did I get here? Why do I keep finding myself in these situations? It's like I'm stuck in a stupid loop, repeating the same mistakes over and over again! I need to break this, but I don't know how.

Sensing the depth of Hope's introspection and the spark of her old spirit, Luna responded with concern and encouragement.

Every experience, Hope, is a stepping stone toward understanding oneself. It's always possible to reflect, learn, and grow. You are the sum of all your experiences: mistakes and successes. Remember: you win some, and you learn some.

Hope couldn't hear Luna, but she felt a pull toward introspection. It was as if the pages of Luna were echoing back to her, urging her to listen to her inner voice. She decided to take a step back from dating. She needed time to heal, reflect, and, most importantly, understand her role in her choices. She began attending therapy, seeking insights into her patterns. Early revelations were like a mirror, reflecting patterns she hadn't seen before.

As Hope delved deeper into her past, she uncovered memories and experiences that had subconsciously influenced her choices. The desire to be loved and validated, stemming from childhood insecurities, often led her to seek relationships that mirrored those feelings of inadequacy.

Dear Luna — I'm beginning to see the patterns, the reasons behind my choices. It's painful, but it's also liberating. I want to break free from this cycle and find a love that's true to who I am.

Feeling the resurgence of Hope's spirit and her journey toward self-awareness, Luna responded.

And Hope heard the faintest whisper. Like a pulse of light through pitch black. Hope's inner voice. Luna. Together.

Embrace this journey of self-discovery, Hope. You are on the path to healing and finding the love that resonates with your true self. It's in you. It starts in you. Stop looking outside for what starts inside.

Hope felt a renewed sense of purpose. Hope was in touch with her accountability. Her past wasn't her fault, but it was now up to her to change it and make something better.

And Luna smiled.

Chapter 9

. . . .

Rediscovery

The realization of her patterns was just the beginning. Hope knew that understanding the problem was one thing, but actively working toward change was another. She needed to rebuild her relationship with herself, to rediscover who she was beyond the confines of romantic relationships.

Dear Luna — For so long, I've defined myself by who I'm with, by how they see me. But who am I really? Who is Hope when she's just... Hope?

Luna responded with gentle encouragement.

Hope, you are a universe unto yourself, filled with dreams, passions, and infinite potential. Rediscover them, embrace them, and let them guide you.

Hope might not have heard Luna's words, but she felt their essence. As a child, Hope loved painting, and she joined an art class to reignite that old passion. As the brush danced on the canvas, memories of her younger self flooded back, reminding her of a time when her identity wasn't tied to someone else.

Hope attended a workshop on self-love and personal growth. It introduced her to the concept of "vision boards." She created one for herself, filling it with images and quotes that resonated with her dreams and aspirations. It served as a daily reminder of who she wanted to be, of the life she wanted to create for herself.

Dear Luna — Today, I added a picture of a solo traveler to my vision board. I've always wanted to travel alone, to explore new places, meet new people. It may be time to make that dream a reality.

Luna, feeling the resurgence of Hope's spirit, whispered back.

Travel will open your eyes and heart, Hope. Embrace the journey, both outside and within.

Hope might not have heard Luna's words, but she felt the importance of a journey of self. Hope took her first solo trip, a backpacking journey across Europe. It was transformative. She met people from different walks of life, each with their own stories and struggles. She learned the value of being alone without feeling lonely and comfortable in her company.

As Hope immersed herself in activities that were about *her* for *her*, she began to see changes in herself. She was more confident, more in tune with her emotions. She learned to set boundaries, to prioritize her well-being.

Dear Luna — I feel like I'm finally coming into my own. I'm learning to love myself, flaws and all. And it's liberating.

Sensing Hope's growth and self-awareness, Luna responded with pride and joy.

You're blossoming, Hope. Embrace this journey of self-love and rediscovery. The best is truly yet to come.

Hope couldn't hear Luna, but she felt proud. And somewhere, in the quiet spaces of Hope's heart, Luna smiled.

Chapter 10

. . . .

Strength

Hope's journey of self-discovery was deeply introspective, but she soon recognized the profound impact of community and shared experiences. There's an inherent strength in unity, in understanding that one's struggles are not solitary, and in drawing wisdom from the journeys of others.

Dear Luna — Today, I attended a women's support group. The stories shared, the resilience on display... it was both heart-wrenching and awe-inspiring. It's remarkable how shared pain can forge such powerful connections.

Luna, always there to guide and comfort, responded softly.

Hope, shared experiences can be powerful bridges. They connect souls, heal wounds, and remind us that we're never truly alone in our struggles.

Hope couldn't hear Luna, but she felt a sense of belonging. Hope encountered women from diverse walks of life in the support group, each narrating tales of heartbreak, resilience, and personal growth. One narrative that deeply touched her was Maya's, a woman who had endured multiple abusive relationships but had risen stronger, channeling her experiences to aid others.

Maya and Hope's bond grew rapidly. They began to spend more time together, attending workshops, hiking, and even indulging in pottery classes. Through Maya, Hope was introduced to a broader circle of formidable, independent women, each navigating their unique journey of self-discovery.

Dear Luna — Maya introduced me to her book club today. We delved into a novel chronicling a woman's journey from adversity to empowerment. The discussions, the myriad perspectives... it was so enlightening. I feel like I'm not merely reading stories but embodying them.

Sensing Hope's growth and the strength she was drawing from her community, Luna whispered back.

Books reflect life, Hope. And just like in stories, every individual you meet adds a chapter to your life's narrative.

Hope couldn't hear Luna, but she felt enriched. This newfound community became Hope's anchor to confidence. They celebrated each other's triumphs, provided solace during challenging times, and consistently uplifted one another. The group organized retreats, immersing themselves in yoga, meditation, and self-growth workshops. They exchanged tales around campfires, danced beneath the starlit sky, and reveled in the pure joy of sisterhood.

Hope also began volunteering at a local women's shelter, channeling her experiences to counsel and uplift those navigating challenging phases. Giving back was therapeutic, imbuing her with a profound sense of purpose.

Dear Luna — Today, at the shelter, a young woman expressed that my journey instilled hope in her. It's astounding how our challenges, our narratives, can serve as beacons for others. I feel like my journey has come full circle.

Luna responded with a mix of pride and warmth.

Your journey, Hope, is a testament to resilience and growth. By sharing your light, you illuminate the paths of others.

Hope couldn't hear Luna, but she felt a deep sense of fulfillment. And Luna, watching over her, felt a surge of pride.

Chapter 11

· · · · · · · · · ·

Nature

Nature possesses a profound ability to heal the soul. The expansive skies, the whisper of leaves, and the rivers' rhythmic flow convey tranquility and introspection. For Hope, the embrace of nature became a haven, a place to rediscover herself and find solace.

Dear Luna — Today, I took a solo hike up the mountain trail. The world seemed boundless as I ascended, and my troubles felt insignificant. Nature has this uncanny ability to offer perspective.

Luna, always attuned to Hope's feelings, responded with gentle wisdom.

Nature and life are so similar, Hope. There are peaks and valleys, storms, and calm. But through it all, there's a beauty and rhythm that reminds us of the bigger picture.

Hope couldn't hear Luna, but she felt a profound connection to the world around her. More and more weekends found Hope venturing into nature. With a backpack slung over her shoulders and hiking boots snugly tied, she'd traverse trails, each step a journey towards understanding herself. The physical exertion of hiking paralleled her emotional odyssey – challenging ascents and moments of weariness, but the panoramic vistas from the summit always justified the journey.

During one weekend, she joined a group for a camping expedition. As they huddled around a campfire beneath the stars, Hope felt an overwhelming bond with the cosmos. The stories exchanged, the melodies sung, and even the simple act of roasting marshmallows added layers to the night's enchantment.

Dear Luna — I feel great! The camping trip was transformative! Removed from the digital noise of daily life,

I genuinely bonded with myself and those around me. The unadulterated beauty of nature, its simplicity... it's rejuvenating!

On a different occasion, Hope ventured into kayaking. Her initial fear of navigating the waters soon gave way to a sense of achievement. Each paddle stroke symbolized her burgeoning confidence and her grit to confront challenges.

Nature also began inspiring her artistry. Hope spent creative time immortalizing the landscapes she encountered in her sketches: tranquil lakes, towering peaks, and verdant woods all vividly portrayed.

Dear Luna — Today, I immortalized the sunrise I witnessed on my recent hike in a painting. The explosion of hues, the dawn of a new day... a poignant reminder that each day heralds a new beginning.

Luna, sensing the depth of Hope's experiences, whispered back.

Nature is a canvas, Hope. It paints lessons of resilience, hope, and renewal. Embrace its teachings and let it guide your soul.

Hope couldn't hear Luna, but she felt invigorated. Through her escapades amidst nature, Hope imbibed invaluable insights. She grasped the essence of persistence, the delight of life's simplicities, and the therapeutic embrace of the natural world. Nature became her sanctuary for introspection, evolution, and tranquility.

Chapter 12

. . . .

Peace

In her quest for healing and clarity, Hope discovered the world of mindfulness and meditation. It began with a workshop she attended, where the instructor spoke about the power of being present and the importance of self-awareness in emotional well-being.

Intrigued, Hope began exploring meditation. Her initial attempts were challenging; her mind wandered, and the weight of her past often intruded on her attempts at finding peace. But with persistence, she started experiencing moments of profound clarity and tranquility.

She established a daily meditation routine, carving out a quiet corner in her home filled with candles, soft cushions, and soothing aromas. This became her sanctuary—a place to retreat from the world and connect with her inner self.

Through meditation, Hope began to understand the patterns of her thoughts and emotions. She learned to observe them without judgment, understanding that they were fleeting and didn't define her. This detachment allowed her to process her past traumas, finding forgiveness and acceptance.

Mindfulness practices extended beyond her meditation sessions. She began practicing mindful eating, savoring each bite, and being present during her meals. She took mindful walks, feeling the earth beneath her feet and the breeze against her skin, appreciating the beauty of the present moment.

Dear Luna — Meditation has opened a new world for me. It's taught me the power of stillness, the beauty of the present, and the impermanence of our emotions. Each session is a journey inward, a chance to reconnect with my true self. Mindfulness has become a way of life, reminding me to cherish each moment, to find joy in the little things, and to embrace life with an open heart.

Luna, sensing the depth of Hope's introspection, responded.

During still moments is when you find your truest self. Continue this journey, Hope, for it leads to inner peace and understanding.

Hope couldn't hear Luna, but she felt a deep, centered quiet.

Chapter 13

. . . .

Return

Hope's love for writing had been a cornerstone of her identity. As a child, she'd penned tales of distant realms, courageous heroines, and enchanting escapades. Her conversations with Luna were filled with dreams, fears, and aspirations, capturing the essence of her youthful spirit. But as life's complexities took over, her once-vibrant dialogue with Luna dimmed, replaced by the noise of self-doubt and external pressures.

One evening, while rummaging through old belongings, Hope rediscovered her journals, filled with her younger self's dialogues with Luna. The pages transported her back, reminding her of the dreams she once shared and the voice she had lost.

Feeling inspired, Hope picked up her pen and began writing again. It started as a therapeutic exercise, pouring out her feelings and reflecting on her past. But as the days passed, her writings transformed into stories of hope, resilience, and self-discovery. She began to weave her experiences into narratives, finding solace in the act of creation. She was conversing, with herself and with Luna, in ways she hadn't for years. Beyond questions and feelings of discontent, Hope was with Luna—just like old times.

Dear Luna — It feels like it's been ages since we've truly connected! Writing has always been my sanctuary, where I can reflect, dream, and heal. With each word, I'm rediscovering my voice, my essence. Sharing my journey has connected me with many, reminding me of the power of stories. Thank you for always being there, even when I lost my way. I'm here and finding my way back to myself.

Luna, feeling the warmth of Hope's renewed spirit, responded.

Welcome home, Love. Your words have always been a reflection of your soul, Hope. Through them, you find clarity, purpose, and connection. Keep writing, for your story is a beacon for many.

Hope couldn't hear Luna, but deep down, she felt reconnected and reaffirmed.

Chapter 14

. . . .

Physical

The bond between the mind and body became increasingly clear to Hope. She realized that her journey of self-discovery wasn't just about emotional healing, but was also about embracing physical wellness.

Dear Luna — Today, I stepped into a Zumba class. Dancing freely, moving to the rhythm, and letting go of all reservations was pure joy!

Luna, feeling Hope's exhilaration, excitedly responded.

Dance, Hope! Let the rhythm of life flow through you, and embrace the joy it brings.

Hope couldn't hear Luna but could feel the positive impact of her exploration into physical wellness. And she diversified. Hope started with yoga, appreciating its blend of physical discipline and mental tranquility. While the initial sessions tested her, she grew to cherish the inner peace it offered. Venturing further, she embraced aerobics, spinning, pilates, and kickboxing. Each activity, with its unique challenges, brought a sense of achievement and a rush of positivity.

Dear Luna — I went running this morning. Feeling the ground beneath my feet, the world around me blurring, and my thoughts clearing... it's a different kind of meditation. It's invigorating.

Luna, sensing Hope's newfound clarity, whispered.

With each step, you're not just moving forward in space, but also in your journey of self-discovery.

Hope couldn't hear Luna but could feel the difference in her balance and mental clarity. Nutrition also became a focal point for Hope. She delved into the world of balanced diets and the benefits of different foods. Her kitchen became a space of experimentation, blending taste with nutrition.

Dear Luna — I tried my hand at a Thai curry tonight. It's fascinating how food can be a source of pleasure and health. I feel rejuvenated.

Luna, with a hint of pride, responded.

Nourish your body, and you nourish your soul. Every meal is a celebration of life.

Hope couldn't hear Luna but could feel her newfound holistic approach to well-being was making a huge difference. Her complexion had a glow, a spring in her step, and a radiance that emanated from within. She learned to appreciate her body, understand its needs, and celebrate its capabilities.

Dear Luna — Today, as I looked at my reflection, I felt a surge of gratitude. Not just for the physical changes, but for the journey, the learnings, and the love I've discovered for myself.

Luna, sensing Hope's holistic growth, responded.

Your body is a reflection of your journey, Hope. Cherish it. Honor it. Continue to grow in love and strength.

Hope couldn't hear Luna, but she felt a deep sense of contentment and pride.

Chapter 15

· · · · · · · · · ·

Connections

Amid her introspective journey, Hope realized that while she had many acquaintances, she had inadvertently distanced herself from Nikki, her closest friend since childhood. The turbulence of her relationships and the emotional whirlwinds had unintentionally created barriers between them.

Dear Luna — I met Nikki today over coffee. It's strange how time can create gaps, even in the most cherished friendships. As we talked, I realized how much I've missed her wisdom, her laughter, and her gentle nudges of reality. I've been so wrapped up in my own world that I forgot the comfort of old friendships. Nikki has this uncanny ability to see through me, to listen without judgment. Sharing with her felt like coming home after a long journey.

Luna, feeling the warmth of Hope's reconnection with Nikki, responded.

Old friends are like stars in our universe, Hope. Even when you don't see them, they're always there, shining for you.

Hope couldn't hear Luna but felt a comforting warmth thinking about her bond with Nikki. Nikki had been a constant in Hope's life. Their shared memories, from childhood scrapes to teenage heartbreaks, were a testament to their enduring bond. They celebrated successes, navigated challenges, and even weathered misunderstandings, always finding their way back to each other.

Hope also found solace and support in Maya, her newfound friend from the self-discovery workshops, as she continued her journey. With her wisdom and shared experiences, Maya became a guiding light for Hope. Their bond, though new, was deep and meaningful. They uplifted each other, shared stories of resilience, and celebrated their individual growth.

Dear Luna — Maya and I attended a seminar today. Her insights and perspective on life are so enlightening. I've always been an old soul, introspective and often lost in thought. Maya, with her vibrant energy and wisdom, brings a balance to my reflective nature. It's incredible how a new friendship can offer so much clarity and support.

Luna, sensing the mutual respect between Hope and Maya, responded.

Every person we meet brings a lesson, Hope. Maya is a testament to the beauty of new beginnings and shared journeys.

Hope couldn't hear Luna but felt invigorated by the support and understanding she found in Maya.

Navigating life's complexities, Nikki and Maya became her pillars of strength. They celebrated achievements, offered constructive feedback, and provided comfort during challenging times. Their shared memories, laughter, and even their disagreements became the foundation of their bonds.

Dear Luna — As Nikki shared a story from her past tonight, I saw so much of myself in her words. It's incredible how two different paths can converge in emotion and experience. With Maya, I'm learning the beauty of shared growth. These friendships, old and new, are teaching me the value of trust, vulnerability, and the sheer joy of connection.

Luna, sensing the depth of Hope's realization, responded.

Friendships, old and new, weave the fabric of our lives, Hope. They remind us of who we were, who we are, and who we aspire to be.

Hope couldn't hear Luna, but she felt a profound sense of belonging and love.

Chapter 16

. . . .

Echoes

The past has a way of resurfacing, often when least expected. For Hope, as she basked in the glow of her newfound self, echoes from her past began reverberating, attempting to pull her back into old patterns.

Dear Luna — Today, out of the blue, I received a message from Brad. It's been so long, yet he brought back a flood of memories with just a few words. He says he misses me. A part of me, the one that remembers the good times, feels a pull to respond. But there's also a voice inside, a wiser one, that wonders if this is just another one of his games. Can the past truly change?

Luna, sensing Hope's dilemma, responded gently.

Hope, the past has its lessons, but the present holds your power. Trust in the wisdom you've gained."

Hope couldn't hear Luna, but she felt peace as she took a moment to contemplate and not simply act. To release and not participate. And Brad's message was just the beginning. Over the next few months, Hope fielded messages and calls from her past relationships. Malcolm reached out, apologizing for his behavior and wanting to reconnect. Andy sent her a long email, reminiscing about their time together and hinting at a second chance. Each message brought with it a whirlwind of emotions. Memories, both sweet and bitter, resurfaced. The familiar tug of old feelings, the what-ifs, and the nostalgia all threatened to pull Hope back into the vortex of her past.

Dear Luna — Last night, I dreamt of Jeff. It was so vivid. We were back in our favorite cafe, the one with the mismatched chairs and the aroma of fresh pastries. We laughed, talked, and everything felt just like old times. I woke up with such a heavy heart, a mix of longing and sadness. Why do these memories from the past keep haunting me, even when I'm trying to move forward?

Luna, with a touch of empathy, whispered back.

Memories are threads in the fabric of your life, Hope. They remind you of where you've been, but they don't dictate where you're going.

Hope couldn't hear Luna, but she felt a profound pride in her growth. All that Hope had uncovered about herself now armed her to confront these past echoes. She recognized them for what they were—remnants of chapters that had closed. With each message, instead of impulsively responding, Hope took a moment to reflect, connect with her inner self, and evaluate her feelings.

Dear Luna — I had a heart-to-heart with Nikki today about all these messages. She listened patiently, as always, and then reminded me of my journey. Of the tears, the growth, the healing, and the transformation I've undergone. It's moments like these that remind me of the power of true friendship. I'm so grateful for friends who keep me grounded, who remind me of my worth when I'm in doubt.

Luna, feeling Hope's gratitude, responded warmly.

Friendships like yours with Nikki are rare gems, Hope. They shine brightest in moments of doubt, guiding you back to your true self.

Hope couldn't hear Luna, but she felt overwhelmed with gratitude. With her friends' support and inner strength, Hope actively acknowledged her past without getting entangled in it. She responded to some messages, expressing gratitude for the memories and setting clear boundaries. To others, she chose not to respond, understanding that silence can sometimes be the most powerful message.

As the echoes from the past faded, Hope emerged stronger, more committed, and with a clearer understanding of her journey. She realized that while the past shapes us, it doesn't define us. Our choices, our actions, and our growth do.

Chapter 17

. . . .

Rebirth

The world around Hope seemed to shimmer with a new vibrancy. Each sunrise brought with it a promise, and every sunset, a gentle reminder of the day's lessons. The woman who once felt lost in the labyrinth of life now walked with a purpose, each step echoing her newfound confidence.

Dear Luna — The world feels so different now. Every morning, I wake up with this sense of clarity, as if I've been handed a new lens through which everything appears brighter and more meaningful. I find myself pausing to appreciate the little things - the chirping of the birds, the warmth of the sun on my skin, the laughter of children playing in the park. It's as though I've rediscovered the beauty in the every day, and in doing so, I've found a deep, resonating peace within myself.

Luna, sensing the profound change in Hope, responded warmly.

Through clarity and self-love, you've painted your world with brighter colors, Hope. Embrace this newfound vision.

Hope couldn't hear Luna, but she felt a profound affirmation. Her home, once a silent witness to her tears and heartaches, now radiated joy. The melodies of her favorite songs filled the air, and her artwork, each piece a testament to her journey, adorned the walls. The void she once felt was filled with her love for herself. She cherished her solitude as a time for reflection and rejuvenation. Mornings grounded her, while evenings became her time of liberation, where she could express herself without bounds.

Dear Luna — I experienced something truly magical during my dance class today. Every movement, every beat, felt like an expression of my soul. I felt so connected to the music, to the rhythm, and, most importantly, to myself. It was as if, through dance, I was celebrating my journey, my growth, and the newfound joy in my heart. This feeling, this overwhelming sense of lightness and freedom, is something I've never felt before, and I cherish every moment of it.

Luna, feeling Hope's elation, replied with enthusiasm.

Dance is the language of the soul, Hope. Through it, you're expressing the joy of your rebirth.

Hope couldn't hear Luna, but she felt invigorated. Her perspective on relationships had evolved. She sought authenticity and recognized her own value. One evening, as she reflected on her journey, an idea blossomed. She wanted to keep growing. On a whim, she signed up for a cooking class, eager for new experiences.

Dear Luna — I took a leap today and signed up for a cooking class. The idea of diving into something completely new, meeting new people, and learning a new skill fills me with excitement and nervousness! But I've realized that growth often lies beyond our comfort zones. So here I am, ready to embrace this new adventure, learn, grow, and add another chapter to my story of self-discovery.

Luna, always supportive, responded with encouragement.

Every new experience is a chapter in your story, Hope. Embrace it, learn from it, and let it add flavor to your life.

Hope couldn't hear Luna, but she felt a surge of excitement. As the days approached for her first class, she was filled with anticipation, unaware of the new lessons life was about to serve her.

Chapter 18

. . . .

Newness

A few days later, the aroma of fresh herbs and spices greeted Hope as she stepped into the cooking studio. The decision to join the class felt right, another step on her journey of self-discovery. The room buzzed with chatter, the clinking of utensils, and the soft hum of ovens preheating. Large wooden tables with cutting boards, bowls, and an array of colorful ingredients stood ready for the activities of new chefs. A flutter of excitement danced in Hope's stomach. This was uncharted territory, a step outside her comfort zone, but she was ready to dive in.

Dear Luna — Today, as I stepped into this cooking studio, I felt like I was entering a new chapter of my life. The energy around me is palpable, and it's not just about the cooking. It's about the stories waiting to be shared, the connections waiting to be made. Tying on this apron reminds me that every new experience is a chance to learn, grow, and discover a part of myself I hadn't known before.

Luna, feeling Hope's exhilaration, responded warmly.

Every new experience is a page in your story, Hope. Embrace it with your enthusiasm, and let your spirit shine.

Hope couldn't hear Luna, but she felt a surge of motivation. As the class commenced, the instructor, a vibrant woman with an evident love for culinary arts, introduced herself and outlined the day's recipe. Hope teamed up with a few others, delving into the world of flavors. She quickly realized that cooking was more than just following a recipe; it was an art, a symphony of ingredients coming together.

Engrossed in her task, Hope began conversing with her tablemates. Their backgrounds varied, but their shared interest in cooking bridged the gaps.

Dear Luna —Today, amidst the scents of spices and the warmth of the stove, I found something more profound.

With Ethan's stories of his travels, Clara's tales of her family's traditional recipes, and Raj's traveled wisdom, I realized that every dish has a story, every flavor a memory. It's not just about the act of cooking, but the stories we share, the memories we create, and the bonds we forge.

Luna, sensing the depth of Hope's realization, whispered back.

Shared passions ignite the most genuine connections, Hope. Cherish these moments of unity.

Hope couldn't hear Luna, but she felt a warmth in her heart. Her new acquaintances were wonderful. Ethan, in particular, caught Hope's attention. His genuine nature and passion for cooking were evident. They exchanged stories about their favorite dishes, culinary disasters, and the joy of discovering new flavors. As they cooked side by side, Hope appreciated Ethan's respectful nature, his willingness to listen, and his shared excitement for the dish they were preparing.

The class flew by, and before she knew it, Hope sat down with her group, savoring the fruits of their labor. The dish was a triumphant medley that danced on the palate. But more than the food, it was the experience, the connections she had made, that left a lasting impression. As they wrapped up, Ethan approached Hope.

"I had a great time cooking with you," he said with a smile. "Would you be interested in joining me for a coffee sometime?"

Hope hesitated momentarily as the echoes of her past relationships briefly invaded her thoughts. But then she remembered her journey, her growth, and the lessons she had learned. She looked into Ethan's eyes, seeing sincerity and kindness.

"I'd love to," she replied, her voice steady and confident.

Dear Luna — Ethan's invitation for coffee brought a mix of emotions. It's not about the coffee but the possibility of a new connection and friendship. I've learned that life is a series of choices, and every option is an opportunity to learn, grow, and embrace the unknown. I'm ready to step into this new chapter with an open heart and mind.

Luna, always supportive, responded with encouragement.

Life is filled with unexpected moments, Hope. Embrace each one, for it adds depth to your journey.

Hope couldn't hear Luna but felt profound gratitude and anticipation for what lay ahead.

Chapter 19

. . . .

Possibilities

The quaint café Ethan had chosen was nestled between two old brick buildings, its entrance adorned with hanging plants and a chalkboard sign that read, "Life is short. Eat dessert first." Inside, the warm glow of string lights illuminated rustic wooden tables and the soft strumming of an acoustic guitar played in the background.

Ethan held the door open for Hope, his eyes meeting hers with a gentle smile. "I thought this place might be to your liking," he said, guiding her to a cozy corner table.

Hope looked around, taking in the ambiance. "It's lovely," she replied, her eyes sparkling with appreciation.

As they settled in, a waitress approached with menus. Ever the gentleman, Ethan asked Hope for her preferences before ordering two coffees and a shared dessert.

The conversation flowed between them. They spoke of their passions and dreams and touched upon past experiences without delving too deep into the wounds.

"So, what drives you, Hope?" he asked, genuinely curious.

Hope paused, collecting her thoughts. "Growth, I'd say," she said. "I've been on a journey of self-discovery, and every day I strive to be a better version of myself. It's not always easy, but it's worth it."

Ethan nodded, his gaze thoughtful. "I admire that. We all have our battles, but it takes courage to face them head-on and evolve."

Dear Luna — Tonight, the surroundings reflected the comforting presence of my company. Ethan's genuine curiosity about my journey has me reflecting deeper on my path. What drives me? It's the pursuit of understanding, growth, and becoming the best version of me that I can be. It's about embracing every lesson, every challenge, and every joy.

Luna paused with silent pride and allowed Hope the space just to *be*.

Hope and Ethan continued to chat, finding common ground in their love for art, nature, and their shared belief in the importance of self-improvement. As the evening progressed, Hope opened up to Ethan in a way she hadn't before: calm, collected, and confident. She didn't feel rushed or infatuated... just engaged, and so was he. Ethan's genuine interest and kind demeanor made her feel valued and heard.

"You know," Hope began, playing with the rim of her coffee cup, "I've learned that relationships reflect where we are on our own personal journeys. It's not about finding someone to live with but someone you can't imagine living without."

Ethan smiled, his eyes softening. "That's beautifully put. And I believe that when two people are in sync with themselves, they can create something extraordinary together."

The evening drew to a close, and as they stepped outside, the cool night air enveloped them. Ethan turned to Hope, his expression sincere. "I had a wonderful time tonight, Hope. I'd love to see you again if you're open to it."

Hope looked up at him, her past fears momentarily clouding her judgment. But then she remembered her growth, her newfound self-worth, and the lessons she had internalized. She took a deep breath and replied, "I'd like that, Ethan."

As they parted ways, Hope felt a mix of excitement and contentment. She knew there were no guarantees in love, but for the first time in a long time, she felt ready to embrace whatever came her way.

Dear Luna — Tonight, I stand at the crossroads of past lessons and future possibilities. The evening with Ethan was a gentle reminder that when you truly value yourself, you open doors to genuine connections and authentic experiences. Here's to the journey ahead, to new beginnings, and to embrace the promise of what's to come.

Luna, ever the guiding light, whispered back.

You're doing it, Hope. You're here. Let go of my hand and take the next step. I'll be here to listen, to love you, and to catch you if you ever fall. But you've got this... and I'm so proud of how far you've come.

Hope couldn't hear Luna, but she felt deep gratitude and hope for the future.

Chapter 19

. . . .

Hope

Hope sat on her balcony, occasionally sipping tea from her favorite cup, as the sun descended to the horizon, casting a golden hue over the city. Luna's pages lay filled with reflections, learnings, and memories of Hope's journey thus far. As she gazed out, lost in thought, she realized that her story wasn't about finding love or escaping toxic patterns. It was about the intricacies of life, a rich combination of joy, pain, growth, and discovery.

Every relationship, every heartbreak, every moment of introspection had added a unique thread to her tapestry. Some threads were dark, representing the pain and challenges she faced. Others were vibrant, symbolizing her moments of joy, self-discovery, and growth. Together, they created a beautiful, complex picture of her life.

Hope understood that life wasn't about seeking a fairy tale ending. It was about embracing every experience, learning from each encounter, and continuously evolving. Relationships aren't about merely finding a person. The right kind of love is about connecting with someone who resonates with your soul and compliments your journey—finding *your* person.

She learned the importance of self-worth and that love wasn't about settling or compromising one's values. It was about mutual respect, understanding, and growth. And most importantly, it was about recognizing that the foundation of any healthy relationship was a strong, self-aware individual.

And Hope put pen to paper.

Dear Luna — As I sit here, reflecting on my journey, I realize love is multifaceted. Finding someone to share life with is part of it. But understanding and embracing oneself, flaws and all... that's what makes love work. Every experience, every relationship, they've been lessons teaching me about myself, the world around me, and how I fit in. I've come to understand that I am a work in progress, constantly evolving and growing. And while I may not be perfect, I am worthy of love and happiness. I am ready to embrace the future, with all its uncertainties, knowing I have the strength and wisdom to face whatever comes my way. Here's to new beginnings, self-love, and endless possibilities that life offers!

Luna responded with warmth and wisdom.

Dear Hope — Your journey has been one of resilience, growth, and self-discovery. You've courageously faced challenges, learned from your experiences, and emerged stronger and wiser. Remember, life is not about the destination but the journey. Embrace every moment, cherish every lesson, and know you are enough. You deserve love, happiness, and all the beautiful things life has to offer. Continue to shine, grow, and inspire. Your story is a testament to the power of self-acceptance and the magic possible when one believes in oneself. Here's to you, Hope, and the beautiful journey ahead of you!

Hope couldn't hear Luna, but she knew Luna was there for her and always had been. For Luna was Hope, and Hope was Luna; each felt a deep sense of peace and contentment, knowing the path before them was filled with happiness, strength, and fulfillment.

Hope took another sip of her tea, picked up her phone... and texted Ethan.

Charles J. Orlando

ABOUT THE AUTHOR

. . . .

Charles J. Orlando has been on a growth path his entire life. He works hard and plays hard. In the mornings, you can usually find him typing away, double cappuccino in-hand at a local coffee shop. In the evenings, catch him on the rooftop with a pre-prohibition cocktail and his girl on his arm, laughing, enjoying life, chatting with people in his community, and learning about what makes people tick.

Charles graduated with high distinction from the University of California, Berkeley, at the tender age of 53—because life, as they say, had other plans. You can find out more about Charles in his upcoming memoir *Spaghetti and Cocaine: Vignettes from a Life Unscripted*, scheduled to be released in 2026. Want more? Visit charlesjorlando.com.

Other Books by Charles J. Orlando

The Problem with Women... is Men®
The Evolution of a Man's Man to a Man of Higher Consciousness

The Problem with Women... is Men®: Volume 2
A Social Media Memoir

The Pact: Goodbye, Past. Hello, Love!

Simple Love Rules: Vol. 1

Don't Date a Dick

Charles J. Orlando

If you've come this far, you must be a curious one. ☺ After all, this is tiny type. Please accept this as your sign from the universe to let go of all the expectations you keep receiving—from others and yourself. Start down a path of self-acceptance and appreciate how far you've come. Be proud! Be bold! And remember: there are clear skies ahead.

Charles J. Orlando

one room press